Retold by Meredith Rusu
Illustrated by the Disney Storybook Art Team

For information address Disney Press, 1101 Flower Street, Glendale, California 91201.
ISBN 978-1-4847-8803-5
FAC-023680-16195

Printed in China
First Hardcover Edition, July 2016
1 3 5 7 9 10 8 6 4 2

For more Disney Press fun, visit www.disneybooks.com
This book was printed on paper created from a sustainable source.

DISNEY
FROZEN
FEVER

BOOK TWO

DISNEY PRESS

Los Angeles • New York

It was early morning in the kingdom of Arendelle, and Queen Elsa was hard at work. It was Anna's birthday. Elsa had been preparing for days. Elsa waved her hands, and a small ice sculpture appeared on the cake she had made. It was pretty, but it didn't seem quite right.

"I just want it to be perfect," Elsa said.

"Check this out!" Kristoff called. He pointed up at a handmade banner he and Sven had made.

Elsa looked at the messy banner. "Kristoff, are you sure I can leave you in charge here?" she asked.

"Absolutely," Kristoff replied.

Suddenly, the kingdom bells began to chime. Like it or not, she would have to trust Kristoff to finish the party preparations.

Up in Anna's bedroom, Elsa found her sister fast asleep.

"Pssst. Anna. Happy birthday!" she whispered.

Anna yawned. "It's my birthday," she mumbled.

As Anna realized what she had just said, she sat up, fully awake. "It's my birthday!" she shouted.

Elsa smiled at her sister. "And it's going to be perfect!" she said.

Elsa gave Anna her first birthday present: a beautiful new green-and-teal dress. With a wave of her hand, Elsa used her magic to add icy sparkles to the dress. She even frosted flowers onto her own gown.

Suddenly, Elsa sneezed. Unseen by Anna and Elsa, two tiny snowmen appeared! The snowmen dropped to the floor and scampered off.

Elsa sniffed and rubbed her nose. "Now come on, you have a birthday to enjoy," she said. Smiling, Elsa handed Anna the end of a string and told her to follow it.

Anna eagerly went wherever the string led. With each stop on the string, she found a present! There was a bracelet, a silly cuckoo clock, and even a painting. Elsa really had thought of everything!

There was only one problem: her sneezing seemed to be getting worse. With each sneeze, more mini snowmen appeared. The snowgies happily scurried off, still unnoticed by the sisters.

Out in the courtyard, Kristoff, Sven, and Olaf were keeping an eye on the surprise party. Suddenly, the little snowmen crashed into the courtyard. The snowgies raced around, knocking over party decorations! Kristoff chased the snowmen. He couldn't let them destroy Anna's party! Olaf, on the other hand, was very excited.

"Little brothers!" he cried happily.

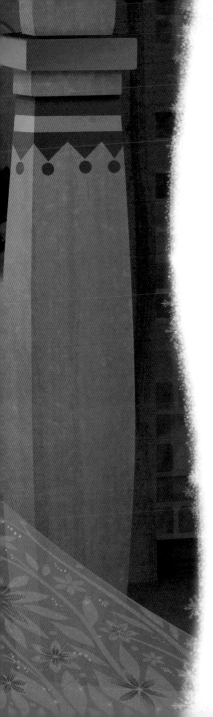

Inside the castle, Anna's
birthday adventure continued.

Anna was having a wonderful
time, but she could tell Elsa was
beginning to feel dizzy. Elsa still
had one gift left! And it was at the
top of Arendelle's clock tower.

At the top, Elsa gave Anna
two beautiful wooden dolls.
They looked just like the sisters—
the perfect birthday present!
Suddenly, Elsa swooned. Anna
caught her sister before she could
fall off the tower.

"Elsa, look at you. You've
got a fever," Anna said, worried.

"I'm sorry, Anna," Elsa said.
"I just wanted to give you one
perfect birthday."

Meanwhile, more snowgies were causing chaos in the courtyard.

One group knocked down Anna's birthday sign. Olaf grabbed the birthday banner and quickly rearranged the letters. But he didn't know how to spell.

"All fixed," Olaf announced, putting up the last piece.

Kristoff tried to read the new banner. "'Dry Banana Hippy Hat'?" It was a disaster!

A second group of snowgies headed for the birthday cake. Kristoff had to think quickly. The snowgies were determined to eat the cake. They launched themselves at it! Kristoff had promised Elsa that he would keep the cake safe, and he refused to let her down. Holding up a bowl, Kristoff blocked the snowgies!

Anna carefully led Elsa back to the castle. As she pushed open the doors to the courtyard, Elsa saw Kristoff, Olaf, and Sven tossing the cake back and forth, trying to keep it away from the snowgies. Anna was focused on Elsa and didn't see anything.

The courtyard was in chaos! Anna looked up just as Kristoff caught the cake and the birthday banner settled into place. Her face lit up. Everything was perfect! But where had all the little snowmen come from?

Kristoff hopped off Sven and walked up to Anna, birthday cake in hand. "Happy birthday," he said. "I love you, baby." For a minute he looked embarrassed. Then he shrugged. "I do." Anna couldn't believe it. It was all so wonderful! But she was still worried about Elsa. After Sven cut slices of cake for everyone, Anna finally led Elsa to bed.

Upstairs, Anna tucked a very tired Elsa into bed. She made her sister some hot soup, sat down next to her, and smiled. "Best birthday present ever," she said.

Elsa was confused. "Which one?"

"You letting me take care of you," Anna replied.

Anna's party was over, but Kristoff and Olaf still had one thing to do. Up in the mountains, they knocked on the doors to the ice palace. Marshmallow answered. Olaf pushed past Marshmallow.

"This way, Sludge and Slush and Slide and Ansel and Flake and Fridge and Flurry and William," he said. Behind Olaf was a long trail of little snowgies.

Kristoff sighed and looked at Marshmallow. "Don't ask," he said.